The
𝔖𝔭𝔬𝔫𝔤𝔢𝔡 𝔖𝔱𝔬𝔫𝔢

Or the Hunt for Christmas Yet-To-Come

By Mike Watt

Cover by Don England

Happy Cloud Media, LLC

The Sponged Stone - Or the Hunt for Christmas Yet-To-Come
First Publication: © Happy Cloud Publishing, 2011
First Happy Cloud Media, LLC Publication © Copyright 2022
Happy Cloud Media, LLC
www.happycloudpictures.net

Originally published in *Phobophobia*, by Mike Watt, 2009

ISBN-13: 978-1-951036-34-8
ISBN-10: 1-951036-34-4

Publisher: Amy Lynn Best
Cover art: Don England
Book design: Ryan Hose

The
Sponged Stone
Or the Hunt for Christmas Yet-To-Come

Marley was dead: to begin with. Dead as a doornail for, by my calendar, over 153 years. But as for old Ebenezer Scrooge, famed gentleman of countless versions of the Dickens' tale, it would seem that he was not. Far from dead, the famous former-miser was sitting across from me in my booth at Shain's, looking very small, very tired, but most alive, and didn't look his age at all.

Not as robust as George C. Scott, though not as wizened as Alistair Sim—and the anthropomorphic opposite of *Uncle Scrooge McDuck*—Mr. Ebenezer Scrooge was a middle-sized, healthy chap, with a rosy glow to his cheeks and nose, due partly to having just come in from the cold and still awaiting his cup of Shain's infamous river-bottom coffee. Having removed and hung up his heavy black overcoat and oddly appropriate silk top hat, Scrooge sat before me, green silk vest upon white silk shirt, single gold ring on left ring finger, and a gleam in his sad pale blue eyes. His face was wrinkled, sagging slightly, looking barely a day over seventy—a complement considering that the gentleman was fast approaching his second century.

In seconds, his coffee arrived, delivered by Shain himself, who smiled at both the old man and me, then left us to our business at hand. Scrooge lifted the chipped cup to his lips, sipped, grimaced, then looked at me with a solemn face. "Mr. Shain tells me that you can help me, Mr. Taz," he said in a surprisingly husky voice. "I would be most grateful to you if you could. There have been many rumored to specialize in unusual cases such as mine, but as you can well understand, they usually turn out to be. . ." he paused for the right word. I took the opportunity to provide it.

"—Humbugs?" I said.

He smiled. "Precisely." Scrooge took another sip of Shain's ghastly concoction, nearly gagging as it slid

down his throat of its own volition.

"Terrible thing to do to innocent coffee beans, isn't it?" I asked, sipping my hot chocolate, my experience-proscribed beverage of choice. Scrooge nodded grimly, glaring at the thick black liquid virtually burbling in his cup.

"Has Shain provided you with the details of my pre-dicament?"

"Not as such, Mr. Scrooge, no." What Shain had done was call me at home, interrupting my umpteenth viewing of *It's a Wonderful Life* with the inquiry "Would you like to meet *the* Ebenezer Scrooge?" Now in my past, I have never once heard of Shain playing Christmas Eve Fools jokes on his friends, and knowing all too well that he only calls with serious business, I ventured out into the lightly falling snow, avoiding main roads choked with last-minute shoppers, and hopped down to his diner, to see just what Shain was going on about.

Scrooge laced his time-gnarled fingers together and leveled his gaze at me. "Well," he began, "without boring you, I trust you've read the story?"

I nodded. "In complete and abridged versions, seen every major film version, and know the *Family Ties* and *Animaniacs* episodes off by heart."

Scrooge winced at the reminder. I guess if my life story had been remade a million times, not to mention parodied, and run back-to-back once a year for a hundred years, I'd be a little sick too. "Well, then you know how it ends. Before the sweetness and light, happily ever after part."

"What specifically?"

"When I turn to Christmas Future and say something like
'Let me sponge away the writing on this stone', or whatever damned fool thing I said."

"Okay."

"Well, when I said that, apparently, I sponged the writing away so completely . . ." he trailed off and splayed his hands.

"So completely you're still alive." I said, stating the obvious for our slower readers.

"Exactly," he said. "The spirits have forgotten about me. Moved on to bigger challenges, I suppose. Like trying to convert Bill Gates or Frank Cowett or something."

"So you want me to try to contact the Christmas Spirits?"

"Just the last one," Scrooge said. "He's probably the only one likely to be of much help."

I thought about this, not entirely sure how to go about doing any of it. But, without any other plans, I was perfectly willing to give it a shot, and said so.

"Thank you, Mr. Taz," Scrooge said. "It would be the perfect Christmas present to a very old man."

Which was, I guess, good enough for me.

*   *   *

And so it came to pass that Caesar Augustus published a decree that had nothing to do with my sitting in my loft on Christmas Eve with Ebenezer Scrooge, thumbing though an ancient book of incantations, trying to figure out how to summon the Ghost of Christmas Yet-To-Come. As I did so, Scrooge sat warming his ancient bones by my roaring fire—which, as I had just built it, was not yet roaring, rather it was more like muttering irritably.

"Do you know how Dickens came to write *A Christmas Carol*?" Scrooge asked.

I looked up from my book, marking my place with my index finger. "No," I said. "And to be honest, I have been sort of wondering. Seeing as it's obviously a true story and all."

"I gave him my story as a Christmas present," he said. "I even gave him some of the money to publish it. He was in the middle of writing installments of *Martin Chuzzlewit*—he was having what he called "The Chuzzlewit agonies", because they weren't selling all that well."

Having read *Martin Chuzzlewit*, I wasn't a bit surprised.

"So on the first time I'd met Charles, we were at a Christmas party at an inn—*The Cock and Bull*, or some damned place—and he told me about all the trouble he was having. Debt up to his eyeballs. So I told him my story, to cheer him up, to tell him that money wasn't everything. He liked it so much, he asked if he could write it down. He was going to give editions as presents to his family. I gave him my blessings, even gave him some money for the printing costs." Scrooge gazed into the fire as he remembered. "Blasted thing has plagued me ever since."

I went back to my book. After a while, my eyes grew tired from reading by little more than firelight and, having no luck anyway, laid the book aside and rubbed my temples. "So, Mr. Scrooge," I began.

"Ebenezer, please."

"Alright. So tell me, Ebenezer, what have you done with yourself all this time?"

"Oh, this and that. Just trying to make people happy, yet keep myself out of the poorhouse. You have no idea how many leeches come out of the woodwork for a handout when they find out that you'll no longer have them arrested for trespassing. Almost went completely broke a couple of times in the beginning."

"I can imagine."

Scrooge grunted. "And when it became obvious that my life span had well surpassed that of "Normal", I thought that I was doubly blessed, and decided to redouble my generous efforts. Making investments that would ensure my purse would always be full should charity call upon me. I became the chief investor in hundreds of companies," he narrowed his gaze and smiled shrewdly at me. "Ever heard of Disneyland?"

"Of course."

"You might not have."

I had to smile admiringly at this.

Scrooge went on. "So year after year, I've raked in my profits, donated to charities, bought orphanages, that sort of thing, changed my name every thirty years or so. Right now people know me as Alan J. Clapsaddle."

I thought about this for a minute. "Yuck," I decided.

Scrooge shrugged. "I'm not overly fond of it myself," he sighed. "But as fulfilling as this doing unto others is, I have to say, quite frankly, that I've gotten too old for this sort of thing." He quickly glanced around. "Don't get me wrong. Giving is good. Really. But I've seen over four lifetimes here on Earth. Over one hundred and ninety Christmases come and gone. Things get better, things get worse. I'd like to pass the torch."

"Do you have children?" I asked. "Grandchildren?"

He nodded. "And dozens of great-grandchildren. All dead." He added. "I've outlived everybody. It is now my turn."

"Wow," I said. And went back to my book. At the end of it, it was suddenly very clear to me that even in the oldest of Harketanian grimoires, there probably isn't a passage useful for specifically invoking the Ghost of Christmas Future. I realized, with a sigh, that I'd have to start at the beginning. And I'd need help from true professionals. Easier said than done, as it was Christmas Eve and even professional witches tend to take the holidays off.

* * *

Regina Delamorte was not, thank God, her real name. But, as a witch's moniker, it was an eye-catcher. But it was hell trying to run her down. Her answering machine wished me Happy Holidays and told me to call back on Tuesday. Her car phone rang for an eternity. Her brother assured me that she was not at his place, and her mother wouldn't tell me anything at all. I finally found her. At Marshall Marshall's Christmas party. An event I was supposed to be attending, which, in the wake of all this Scrooge business, I'd forgotten about.

I apologized to Marshall, who, in his partially saturated state, not only couldn't care less that I wasn't there, was apparently unaware of my absence; he went and fetched Gina, who was none too happy to have her rejoicing and Noel-ing interrupted.

I explained the situation to her.

There was a long pause on the other end of the phone. I suspected a season-inspired insult pending. "Taz," she began. "You've been hitting the eggnog a bit hard tonight, haven't you?"

Do I know my colleagues or what?

"Gina, do you think you can slip away for a minute?"

"Taz, there is no way in Hell I am leaving this party. It's bad enough you've forced me to give my spot under the mistletoe."

"I'm not asking you to leave the party. Can you slip into the bedroom or the bathroom for ten minutes? I need you to try and find that ghost for me."

"The Ghost of Christmas Future?"

"Right."

"The one that looks like a low-rent version of the grim reaper?"

"Usually, though it depends on what film you're watching."

"You want me to post-pone my regaling so that

you can play Ebenezer Scrooge?"

"This is *for* Ebenezer Scrooge. Try to pay attention, will you?"

There was another long pause. I tried to speed her up with "Can you just humor me, please?"

I was answered with: "You're gonna owe me big for this."

"Wait 'til you see what I got you for Christmas," I replied, making a mental note to rush out as soon as the stores opened on Tuesday. "Call me at my place as soon as you can whether you've located it or not."

I hung up and clapped my hands together, turning to my guest. "Well," I began. "Gina's going to try to cut to the chase. She's a more experienced summoner than I am. In the mean time, we're going to go a different route."

"What do you have in mind?" Scrooge asked.

"Well, just in case he's busy, I'm going to give Marley a shot."

Scrooge stared at me. "Marley? Why? What does Marley have to do with this?"

I shrugged. "He knew what was going on last time, didn't he?"

"I suppose."

"Well it's better than sitting around watching *Miracle on 34th Street* waiting for Gina to call."

"No it isn't."

"Richard Attenborough version," I replied.

"I wonder how old Jacob is doing." said Scrooge.

*   *   *

Jacob Marley was still in chains when I found him, though they had decreased to the size of paper clips and didn't look nearly as cumbersome. He was still a frightful sight, and looked shockingly like Sir Alec Guinness from *Scrooge*, right down to the kerchief tied around his head to keep his jaw from flopping open. He stood hovering in the center of the room, a bluish mist barely remaining in man-form, glinting slightly in the firelight. Through him, I could see my Christmas
tree and its irregularly blinking lights.

"Scrooge," he moaned, the air rushing through him like a wind through a tunnel. "*Scrooooooge.*"

"H-hello, Jacob," Scrooge said, forcing a smile. "How have you been?"

Marley grinned. "Can't complain." He crossed his legs and sat in mid-air.

"Your burden has lessened, I see."

"Oh, yes. Not as heavy, though I miss the clanking and rattling."

"You do?"

"Mmmhmm. I used to do some part-time haunting when they were really impressive. Now all they're good for are slightly eerie wind chimes around Halloween," He rested chin in palm and elbow on transparent knee. "So," he said. "How's by you?"

"Not bad, Jacob."

"How's the family?"

"Dead, thanks."

Marley blinked. "Dead? Say, how long's it been anyway?"

"About a hundred and forty-nine years," Scrooge replied. "Give or take."

"Good Heavens!" Marley exclaimed. "And you're still here. Or rather *there*? On Earth?"

"I'm afraid so."

"How can this be? Do the spirits know about this?"

"That's what we called you to find out," I said. Marley

swiveled his head and stared at me, bug-eyed.

"Who the devil are you?"

"Uh, Jefferson Taz. Your summoner."

"Oh. Well, that would explain the pentagram I'm standing over." He said, more to himself, I suppose.

"Yes, it would."

"You know," Marley said. "I've never been summoned before. I wasn't even aware that that was what was happening."

"It is occasionally a subtle process," I agreed, though without much conviction having never undergone a summoning myself.

"Well, since I'm here, what can I do for you Ebenezer?"

"Well, Jacob, we called you to see if you had any

idea, er, why I'm still alive."

Regretfully, Marley shook his head. "I'm afraid not, Ebenezer, no. The spirits don't keep much contact with me since you've changed your ways. Good change, too, Ebenezer. One-hundred-and-eighty degrees without quite altering your integrity. Quite a tightrope walk that. Why I've seen men change their ways only to get stepped on for the rest of their lives, but not you," Marley paused, seeing the puzzled look on Scrooge's face. "Oh, I kept an eye on you for a time afterward.
Just to make sure you didn't get out of hand."

"Er, thank you, Jacob."

"Think nothing of it, Ebenezer."

"Um, not to be a Grinch, fellas. But we really should get going here. Christmas Eve is dwindling and I've got family to visit
tomorrow."

"My apologies, Taz," Scrooge said. "Jacob, would you know where Future might be?"

Marley thought for a second, pressing the tip of his index finger to his temple and cocking his head,

still hovering over the floor. "Hmmm. No, can't say as I do, Ebenezer. But if I run into him, I'll be sure to let him
know you're looking for him."

"Er, is there much chance you'll be running into him soon, Jacob?"

"Uh, not really, no. Sorry, Ebenezer. We don't really travel in the same circles. But you never can tell. But I'll keep an eye out. I'll tell you what though, he's usually best reached around the time when the clock strikes three, remember?"

"All too vividly. And when it strikes four, he turns into a bed post."

Marley blinked. "Does he really?"

"He did last time."

"Well that's certainly a neat trick. Next time I see him, I'll have to get him to teach it too me." Marley began to fade away, waving as he did so. "My time is done. Merry Christmas,
Ebenezer. Merry Christmas you odd looking young man."

"Merry Christmas, Jacob."

I grunted.

"And a Happyyy Newwww Yearrrrrr."

Scrooge sighed when Marley was gone. "Well, that was uneventful," he said.

"And melodramatic towards the end," I added with a

hint of disgust. "He really should get with the times. Ghosts don't moan anymore. They just fiddle with your appliances, and blank out your e-mail." I glanced up at the clock. Five minutes to two am. Boy, this had been a long night already. Legally, it was Christmas Day. At least it was following the time-line of the story. "Two am is Christmas Present's allotted time, isn't it?"

"Last time I checked," said Scrooge.

Just to make sure, I flipped on the tube. On one of the local channels, the Henry Winkler version was playing. They were still in Christmas Past. "Now *she* was a dull spirit," said Scrooge.

"Who?" I said.

"Past. No sense of humor at all."

At two am exactly, my phone rang. It was Gina.

"I got something," she said, though I'm not sure if he's who you're looking for. He's the hit of the party, though. Brought all his

own food. Filled the room. Here, I'll put him on."

Though she was a bit sloshed, I had a hunch I knew who she was talking about. In seconds a deep voice was booming in my ear over the phone. "Come in and know me better, Man! Or should I say, come *over*. The party's just getting started."

"No prior commitments this year I see."

"Who is it?" said Scrooge at my elbow. I punched the speaker button on my phone and the room flooded with the cross-town voice of the Spirit of Christmas Present.

"Nothing that cannot wait until the wine is drunk and all are Merry!" said the voice, with a slight slur in its earth-shaking voice.

"Without keeping you from anything, Spirit," I said, shouting slightly so as to be heard over the rap version of "Silent Night" flooding the speakers in the background. "Would you happen to know where your third party is?"

"Christmas Yet-to-Come you mean?"

"That's the one. Any idea where he might be lurking."

"Absolutely! Are you sure you wouldn't rather join us,

Man? The cornucopia overflowing."

"Thanks just the same, but I really have to find Future."

"That killjoy!" came the contemptuous equivalent of a thunderous mutter. "Yes, he's out and about, showing the wicked their individual fates. Not much trick in that: take them to a church yard, point at a tombstone. No real flair. No fun. He's always like that. Work, work, work."

"I agree. He should relax. Now, where might he be?"

"Try 112 South Graham Street. Apartment C," said Present. "Unless he's already turned into a bedpost there—" I shot a glance at Scrooge. "—In which case he's at 417 East Carson. Number 8. After that, I'm not sure. He sure as hell won't be here, I can tell you that! Oh, never. He's much too good for the likes of us."

"Thanks very much, Spirit. Put Gina back on." As he handed the phone over, I heard Marshall's distinctive air-raid siren doorbell. And immediately followed: "Come in and know me better, Man!" I shook my head to clear out the ringing church bells. "Gina! I really owe you one!"

"Don't worry about it, Taz," she sloshed. "Th' guy's a ton of laughs. Even brought *Pictionary* with him." She laughed uproariously at this. I could tell that Miss Delamorte was just chock *full* of Christmas Cheer.

"Well, thanks anyway. Wish Marshall a Merry Christmas, or a Happy Hanukkah, or whatever faith he is this week."

I hung up. Grabbed Scrooge and together we raced out into the gently falling snow.

* * *

At this time, the gently falling snow was falling less than gently. The sky was white with the Cold Miser's latest tantrum. Jack Frost was wreaking havoc, almost literally seizing my nose with both fists. At this point, I should explain that the heater in my modest little economy car is a little fussy. It doesn't like the cold. The easiest way to heat up my car is to get in, let it run for a little while, then drive someplace warm.

My road gets excellent plow service. Due to this excellent plow service, it took ten minutes to dig my car out of the solid snow bank that had formed around it. And by the time we were out, and had done a few three-sixties on the side-road shortcuts, we arrived too late 312 South Graham. All we found there was a tall skinny guy running through the streets without a coat wishing every fire hydrant and adult theater a Merry Christmas.

So I threw my humble car into gear—pissing it off royally in the process—and we sped off, laughing all the way, to 317 E. Carson. Number 8.

Panting, sliding and slipping, Scrooge and I ran as fast as we could through the deep snow, trying desperately to prevent our bare skin from coming in contact with the metal railing as we hurried up the icy steps to the apartment building. After a moment of panic, we found the appropriate buzzer and pressed it.

We waited. Scrooge stabbed a crooked finger at the buzzer again. We waited some more. Just as we were about to take a flying leap through the glass, a timid little voice came over the box. "Y-yes? Who's there?"

"Mr.—" (I found the name). "Garnet?" I said. "There's no time to explain. Is there somebody in there with you?"

There was a pause that seemed to last until Groundhog's Day. "Er, sort of. Sort of somebody."

"Please let us in. We have to see him."

"Don't let him turn into a hat rack or anything until we get there."

"Oh. Okay."

The buzzer sounded; we threw open the door and raced inside. Being an old, tired man who'd waited a long time for this moment, Scrooge beat me up the stairs by a full flight and a half, leaving me panting and winded on the sixth floor. Wheezing, I dragged myself into Number 8 by my fingertips. Garnet, a thin, nervous looking man held the door for me. "Jefferson Taz," I said and looked around for Scrooge.

I saw him for just a minute. I swear, I think it was a minute exactly. Scrooge was standing, cane and hat in hand, before the tallest, most solid looking apparition I'd ever seen. It was exactly as the story had described right down to the skeletal hands: an ash-grey shroud covering darkness, a pool of half-glimpsed light worn as a curtain. It towered over Scrooge, who clutched its hem. Behind him, a headstone had materialized, with EBENEZER SCROOGE etched into its surface. The writing, it seem, was unsponged.

There were tears in Scrooge's eyes as he pressed the Spirit's hem to his cheek. With a sob, he looked over his shoulder at me and smiled. "Thank you, Mr. Taz. Thank you so very much."

"Merry Christmas, Mr. Scrooge," I replied.

"Merry Christmas."

And with that, the Spirit of Christmas Yet-To-Come and Ebenezer Scrooge vanished entirely from the living room of Mr. Henry Garnet.

When we were alone at last, without a headstone containing *anyone's* name, Henry Garnet turned to me. "Merry Christmas," he said, without knowing anything else to say.

"Merry Christmas," I returned.

"Was that *the* Ebenezer Scrooge?" He asked in a small voice.

"Yep."

"Oh."

We stood there for a moment. Two strangers on a very early Christmas Day. "They did it one night," Garnet said after a while. "They did it all."

I nodded. What else could I say. "Well, good night," I said and turned to go.

"Wait," he said. I turned back. "Just a second." He went to the couch. Next to the couch was an open window. Beneath the window was East Carson St., which was the main thoroughfare for this end of town. "Here," he said as he turned back. In his hand was a semi-automatic rifle, complete with a sight.

He handed it to me, stock and all. "I hadn't loaded it yet. I was going to do that tonight. Before they came." He smiled. There were tears in his eyes. "I don't have to now. I never had to really." He shrugged. "Well, good night. Merry Christmas," He said as he closed the door behind me.

I stood in the hallway of Garnet's building, looking down at the rifle I held in both hands. The spirits had done it in one night, I saw. I felt like I had been given a gift too.

Happy Holidays

from Happy Cloud Media!

ABOUT THE AUTHOR: Mike Watt is a writer, journalist and screenwriter. He is the author of the short fiction collection, *Phobophobia*, the novels *The Resurrection Game* and *Suicide Machine*, and from McFarland Publishing: *Fervid Filmmaking: 66 Cult Pictures of Vision, Verve and No Self-Restraint*. He is the author of the *Movie Outlaw* book series, and editor-in-chief of the cult film magazine *Exploitation Nation*. With Amy Lynn Best, they founded the production company, Happy Cloud Pictures, and he has written and produced or directed the award-winning feature film *The Resurrection Game, as well as Splatter Movie: The Director's Cut, A Feast of Flesh, Demon Divas and the Lanes of Damnation* and the award-winning *Razor Days.*

ABOUT THE ARTIST: Donald England is a Michigan based artist specializing in creepy and macabre art for the last 25 years. He is a product of late-night eighties television and comic book shops. In the nineties, he co-created the comic Lethal Lita with Michael Leblanc, and worked on other comics like *Tales from the Ravaged Lands*. By the end of the nineties, he was primarily working on horror projects, creating catalog cover art for VHS sellers like *Video Wasteland* and *Video Dungeon*. Over the years, his work has been seen in a number of magazines like *Horror* Hound and *Liquid Cheese*, as well as cover art for *Evilspeak*. His art has been featured in *Late Night Snack, The Thing* and *Stranger Things* art books, Deadworld, Cromwell Green, and on the covers of *Erie Tales, A Fistfull of Dead Folk*, and *Night Pie*ces. Visit www.donaldengland.com

ALSO FROM HAPPY CLOUD PUBLISHING:
www.happycloudpublishing.com

Night of the Living Dead 1990: The Version You've Never Seen
by Tom Savini

Shadows & Light: Journeys With Outlaws in Revolutionary Hollywood
by Gary Kent

Splatter Movie: The Director's Cut – Annotated Screenplay
by Amy Lynn Best

Nightmare Pavilion and Other Supernatural Tales by Andy

Rausch

The Shatter Dead Collection by Scooter McCrae

Sixteen Tongues – Annotated Screenplay by Scooter McCrae

Phobophobia by Mike Watt

The *Movie Outlaw* Series by Mike Watt